Lady Lupin's Book of Etiquette

Babette Cole

For Lady Lupir Longtail
(Royal Dog of Scotland)
and
her lovely puppies

HAMISH HAMILTON LTD

Published by the Penguin Group
Penguin Books Ltd, 80 Strand, London WC2R 0RL, England
Penguin Putnam Inc., 375 Hudson Street, New York, New York 10014, USA
Penguin Books Australia Ltd, 250 Camberwell Road, Camberwell, Victoria 3124, Australia
Penguin Books Canada Ltd, 10 Alcorn Avenue, Toronto, Ontario, Canada M4V 3B2
Penguin Books India (P) Ltd, 11 Community Centre, Panchsheel Park, New Delhi – 110 017, India
Penguin Books (NZ) Ltd, Cnr Rosedale and Airborne Roads, Albany, Auckland, New Zealand
Penguin Books (South Africa) (Pty) Ltd, 24 Sturdee Avenue, Rosebank 2196, South Africa

Penguin Books Ltd, Registered Offices: 80 Strand, London WC2R 0RL, England

www.penguin.com

First published 2001
3 5 7 9 10 8 6 4 2

Copyright © Babette Cole, 2001

The moral right of the author/illustrator has been asserted

Set in Monotype Baskerville

Printed in Italy by L.E.G.O.

British Library Cataloguing in Publication Data
A CIP catalogue record for this book is available from the British Library

ISBN 0–241–14096–X

This edition produced for The Book People Ltd,
Hall Wood Avenue, Haydock, St Helens WA11 9UL

Lady Lupin's Book of Etiquette

Babette Cole

TED SMART

"Now that you are growing up," said Lady Lupin to her puppies,

"it is time to learn about
'ETIQUETTE'."

"What does that mean,
dear Mother?"
said
Lady Lobelia.

"How to behave like
ladies and gentledogs
so that all will love you,"
said Lady Lupin.

"It may even help you
to get a good
mate!"

"For instance, do not squabble over
your bones,

but say, 'Please pass the bones, dear brother.'

'Of course, Lobelia.'

'Thank you so much, Luchie!'

At dinner, never serve yourself first.

side plate and butter knife

pudding spoon

and fork

DINNER PLATE

wine glass

This is how your place is set.

MEAT

FISH

1st COURSE

SOUP

Oysters are eaten raw from the shell...

with lemon juice.

Spaghetti is eaten with a fork only.

Use a spike and tongs
for snails.

You need crackers
to eat lobster.

Never bark with your mouth full!

Or leave the
table…

without asking permission!

Try not to show off at parties!

woof   woof   woof   woof   woof   woof   woof   woof

Always send thank-you letters.

Longtail Castle,
Lochbone,
Scotland.

Lady Snoutover,
Pedegree Park,
Pawshire,

20th Sept. 2001

Dear Lady Snoutover,
Thank you so much for your party last Saturday. I enjoyed it enormously.
Yours Sincerely,
Lady Lobelia Longtail

Never ask an older lady her age!

sssnarl!

Remember, 'Ladies always go first!'

Ladies' hats
with veils
should be avoided by messy eaters!

Shake paws correctly.

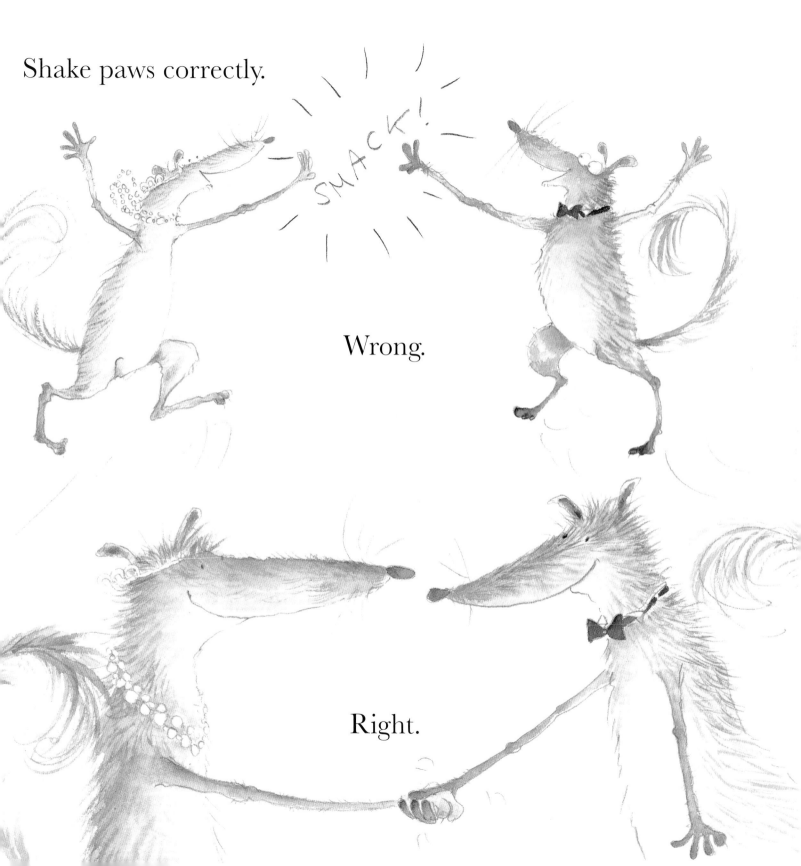

SMACK!

Wrong.

Right.

Remember to open doors for older dogs.

And offer them a seat!

It's easier to say sorry in writing.

Longtail Ca[...]
Lochbone,
Scotland.

The Earl of Earwig,
Fleascastle,
Great Itchington,
Sussex.

21st Sept. 2001

Dear Lord Earwig,
I really am most awfully sorry
for causing your fall at Longtail
Castle yesterday. Please accept
my apologies.
Yours very Sincerely,
Lady Lobelia Longtail.

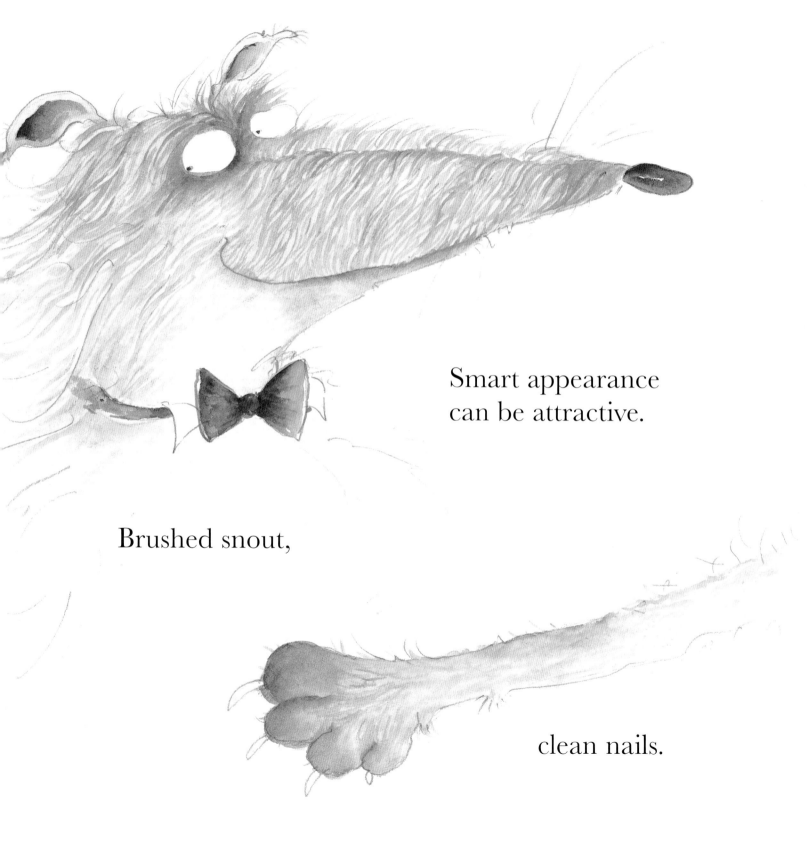

Smart appearance
can be attractive.

Brushed snout,

clean nails.

Too much make-up may give an unsuitable impression

… and could attract the wrong mate!

Oh really,
Lobelia!

Above all, always remain calm when
faced with the
unexpected!"

Some other books by Babette Cole

THE BAD GOOD MANNERS BOOK
BAD HABITS!
KING CHANGE-A-LOT
PRINCE CINDERS
PRINCESS SMARTYPANTS
WINNI ALLFOURS

Babette Cole was born in Jersey, in the Channel Islands. She attended a convent school where she seemed to spend most of her time telling stories and drawing pictures. She graduated from Canterbury College of Art in 1973 and has been a writer and illustrator ever since.
Her first book was published in 1976.
Babette Cole lives on a stud farm in Lincolnshire, UK, where she breeds Show Hunters.
She rides and competes side-saddle and was Side-Saddle Rider of the Year in 1998.
She has two Norfolk terriers and three Scottish deerhounds, including the ones that appear in this story – Lady Lupin, Lobelia and Luciano.
For part of the year she lives in the British Virgin Islands, where she does a good deal of work and sailing. Babette says she does not set out to make her books unconventional –
"They just happen that way!"